This Feelings Journal Belongs To:

_____ Mcrices arrc _____

My Feelings Journal © 2019 by Matilda Boyd

First edition: 2019

Dear _____,

  ...ay I feel _____

because _____

_____

_____

_____

_____

_____

_____

_____

_____

_____

_____

_____

_____

*The back of this page is left blank so that you can draw a picture of
how you feel and tear this page out of your journal to give someone
your message.

Dear _____,

Today I feel _____

because _____

_____

_____

_____

_____

_____

_____

_____

_____

_____

_____

_____

_____

*The back of this page is left blank so that you can draw a picture of how you feel and tear this page out of your journal to give someone your message.

Date: _____

Today I feel _____.

This is a picture of how I'm feeling today ...

I feel this way because ...

_____

_____

_____

_____

_____

_____

Something that might help me feel better is ...

_____

_____

_____

_____

_____

_____

Picture of me doing this ...

Someone who I would like to share my

feelings with is _____.

I will do this by talking to them / writing

them a note. (Circle one)

Dear _____,

Today I feel _____

because _____

_____

_____

_____

_____

_____

_____

_____

_____

_____

_____

_____

_____

*The back of this page is left blank so that you can draw a picture of how you feel and tear this page out of your journal to give someone your message.

Date: _____

Today I feel _____.

😊 😍 😜 😟 😢 😬 😠

This is a picture of how I'm feeling today ...

I feel this way because ...

_____

_____

_____

_____

_____

_____

_____

Something that might help me feel better is ...

_____

_____

_____

_____

_____

_____

Picture of me doing this ...

Someone who I would like to share my

feelings with is _____.

I will do this by talking to them / writing

them a note. (Circle one)

Dear _____,

Today I feel _____

because _____

_____

_____

_____

_____

_____

_____

_____

_____

_____

_____

_____

*The back of this page is left blank so that you can draw a picture of how you feel and tear this page out of your journal to give someone your message.

Date: _____

Today I feel _____.

This is a picture of how I'm feeling today ...

I feel this way because ...

_____

_____

_____

_____

_____

_____

Something that might help me feel better is ...

_____

_____

_____

_____

_____

_____

Picture of me doing this ...

Someone who I would like to share my

feelings with is _____.

I will do this by talking to them / writing

them a note. (Circle one)

Dear _____,

Today I feel _____

because _____

_____

_____

_____

_____

_____

_____

_____

_____

_____

_____

_____

_____

The back of this page is left blank so that you can draw a picture of
ow you feel and tear this page out of your journal to give someone
jour message.

Date: _____

Today I feel _____.

This is a picture of how I'm feeling today ...

I feel this way because ...

_____

_____

_____

_____

_____

_____

_____

Something that might help me feel better is ...

_____

_____

_____

_____

_____

_____

Picture of me doing this ...

Someone who I would like to share my

feelings with is _____.

I will do this by talking to them / writing

them a note. (Circle one)

Dear _____,

Today I feel _____

because _____

_____

_____

_____

_____

_____

_____

_____

_____

_____

_____

_____

_____

*The back of this page is left blank so that you can draw a picture of how you feel and tear this page out of your journal to give someone your message.

Date: _____

Today I feel _____.

😊 😍 😜 😟 😢 😬 😠

This is a picture of how I'm feeling today ...

I feel this way because ...

_____

_____

_____

_____

_____

_____

Something that might help me feel better is ...

_____

_____

_____

_____

_____

_____

Picture of me doing this ...

Someone who I would like to share my

feelings with is _____.

I will do this by talking to them / writing

them a note. (Circle one)

Dear _____,

Today I feel _____

because _____

_____

_____

_____

_____

_____

_____

_____

_____

_____

_____

_____

_____

*The back of this page is left blank so that you can draw a picture of how you feel and tear this page out of your journal to give someone your message.

Date: _____

Today I feel _____.

This is a picture of how I'm feeling today ...

I feel this way because ...

_____

_____

_____

_____

_____

_____

Something that might help me feel better is ...

_____

_____

_____

_____

_____

_____

Picture of me doing this ...

Someone who I would like to share my

feelings with is _____.

I will do this by talking to them / writing

them a note. (Circle one)

Dear _____,

Today I feel _____

because _____

_____

_____

_____

_____

_____

_____

_____

_____

_____

_____

_____

_____

The back of this page is left blank so that you can draw a picture of how you feel and tear this page out of your journal to give someone your message.

Date: _____

Today I feel _____.

This is a picture of how I'm feeling today ...

I feel this way because ...

_____

_____

_____

_____

_____

_____

_____

Something that might help me feel better is ...

_____

_____

_____

_____

_____

Picture of me doing this ...

Someone who I would like to share my

feelings with is _____.

I will do this by talking to them / writing

them a note. (Circle one)

Dear _____,

Today I feel _____

because _____

_____

_____

_____

_____

_____

_____

_____

_____

_____

_____

_____

_____

*The back of this page is left blank so that you can draw a picture of
how you feel and tear this page out of your journal to give someone
your message.

Date: _____

Today I feel _____.

This is a picture of how I'm feeling today ...

I feel this way because ...

_____

_____

_____

_____

_____

_____

Something that might help me feel better is ...

_____

_____

_____

_____

_____

_____

Picture of me doing this ...

Someone who I would like to share my

feelings with is _____.

I will do this by talking to them / writing

them a note. (Circle one)

Dear _____,

Today I feel _____

because _____

_____

_____

_____

_____

_____

_____

_____

_____

_____

_____

_____

_____

*The back of this page is left blank so that you can draw a picture of how you feel and tear this page out of your journal to give someone your message.

Date: _____

Today I feel _____.

😊 😍 😜 😟 😢 😁 😠

This is a picture of how I'm feeling today ...

I feel this way because ...

_____

_____

_____

_____

_____

_____

Something that might help me feel better is ...

_____

_____

_____

_____

_____

_____

Picture of me doing this ...

Someone who I would like to share my

feelings with is _____.

I will do this by talking to them / writing

them a note. (Circle one)

Dear _____,

Today I feel _____

because _____

_____

_____

_____

_____

_____

_____

_____

_____

_____

_____

_____

*The back of this page is left blank so that you can draw a picture of
how you feel and tear this page out of your journal to give someone
your message.

Date: _____

Today I feel _____.

This is a picture of how I'm feeling today ...

I feel this way because ...

_____

_____

_____

_____

_____

_____

_____

Something that might help me feel better is ...

_____

_____

_____

_____

_____

_____

Picture of me doing this ...

Someone who I would like to share my

feelings with is _____.

I will do this by talking to them / writing

them a note. (Circle one)

Dear _____,

Today I feel _____

because _____

_____

_____

_____

_____

_____

_____

_____

_____

_____

_____

_____

_____

*The back of this page is left blank so that you can draw a picture of
how you feel and tear this page out of your journal to give someone
your message.

Date: _____

Today I feel _____.

This is a picture of how I'm feeling today ...

I feel this way because ...

_____

_____

_____

_____

_____

_____

Something that might help me feel better is …

_____

_____

_____

_____

_____

_____

Picture of me doing this …

Someone who I would like to share my

feelings with is _____.

I will do this by talking to them / writing

them a note. (Circle one)

Dear _____,

Today I feel _____

because _____

_____

_____

_____

_____

_____

_____

_____

_____

_____

_____

_____

*The back of this page is left blank so that you can draw a picture of
how you feel and tear this page out of your journal to give someone
your message.

Date: _____

Today I feel _____.

This is a picture of how I'm feeling today ...

I feel this way because ...

_____

_____

_____

_____

_____

_____

Something that might help me feel better is ...

_____

_____

_____

_____

_____

_____

Picture of me doing this ...

Someone who I would like to share my

feelings with is _____.

I will do this by talking to them / writing

them a note. (Circle one)

Dear _____,

Today I feel _____

because _____

_____

_____

_____

_____

_____

_____

_____

_____

_____

_____

_____

_____

*The back of this page is left blank so that you can draw a picture of
how you feel and tear this page out of your journal to give someone
your message.

Date: _____

Today I feel _____.

😊 😍 😜 😟 😢 😬 😠

This is a picture of how I'm feeling today ...

I feel this way because ...

_____

_____

_____

_____

_____

_____

_____

Something that might help me feel better is ...

_____

_____

_____

_____

_____

_____

Picture of me doing this ...

Someone who I would like to share my

feelings with is _____.

I will do this by talking to them / writing

them a note. (Circle one)

Dear _____,

Today I feel _____

because _____

_____

_____

_____

_____

_____

_____

_____

_____

_____

_____

_____

*The back of this page is left blank so that you can draw a picture of
how you feel and tear this page out of your journal to give someone
your message.

Date: _____

Today I feel _____.

This is a picture of how I'm feeling today ...

I feel this way because ...

_____

_____

_____

_____

_____

_____

Something that might help me feel better is ...

_____

_____

_____

_____

_____

_____

Picture of me doing this ...

Someone who I would like to share my

feelings with is _____.

I will do this by talking to them / writing

them a note. (Circle one)

Dear _____,

Today I feel _____

because _____

_____

_____

_____

_____

_____

_____

_____

_____

_____

_____

_____

_____

*The back of this page is left blank so that you can draw a picture of how you feel and tear this page out of your journal to give someone your message.

Date: _____

Today I feel _____.

😊   🥰   😜   😟   😢   😬   😠

This is a picture of how I'm feeling today ...

I feel this way because ...

_____

_____

_____

_____

_____

_____

_____

Something that might help me feel better is ...

_____

_____

_____

_____

_____

_____

Picture of me doing this ...

Someone who I would like to share my

feelings with is _____.

I will do this by talking to them / writing

them a note. (Circle one)

Dear _____,

Today I feel _____

because _____

_____

_____

_____

_____

_____

_____

_____

_____

_____

_____

_____

_____

*The back of this page is left blank so that you can draw a picture of how you feel and tear this page out of your journal to give someone your message.

Date: _____

Today I feel _____.

This is a picture of how I'm feeling today ...

I feel this way because ...

_____

_____

_____

_____

_____

_____

Something that might help me feel better is ...

_____

_____

_____

_____

_____

_____

Picture of me doing this ...

Someone who I would like to share my

feelings with is _____.

I will do this by talking to them / writing

them a note. (Circle one)

Dear _____,

Today I feel _____

because _____

_____

_____

_____

_____

_____

_____

_____

_____

_____

_____

*The back of this page is left blank so that you can draw a picture of
how you feel and tear this page out of your journal to give someone
your message.

Date: _____

Today I feel _____.

This is a picture of how I'm feeling today ...

I feel this way because ...

_____

_____

_____

_____

_____

_____

Something that might help me feel better is ...

_____

_____

_____

_____

_____

_____

Picture of me doing this ...

Someone who I would like to share my

feelings with is _____.

I will do this by talking to them / writing

them a note. (Circle one)

Dear _____,

Today I feel _____

because _____

_____

_____

_____

_____

_____

_____

_____

_____

_____

_____

_____

_____

The back of this page is left blank so that you can draw a picture of
how you feel and tear this page out of your journal to give someone
your message.

Date: _____

Today I feel _____.

This is a picture of how I'm feeling today ...

I feel this way because ...

_____

_____

_____

_____

_____

_____

_____

Something that might help me feel better is ...

_____

_____

_____

_____

_____

_____

Picture of me doing this ...

Someone who I would like to share my

feelings with is _____.

I will do this by talking to them / writing

them a note. (Circle one)

Dear _____,

Today I feel _____

because _____

_____

_____

_____

_____

_____

_____

_____

_____

_____

_____

_____

*The back of this page is left blank so that you can draw a picture of how you feel and tear this page out of your journal to give someone your message.

Date: _____

Today I feel _____.

This is a picture of how I'm feeling today ...

I feel this way because ...

_____

_____

_____

_____

_____

_____

Something that might help me feel better is ...

_____

_____

_____

_____

_____

_____

Picture of me doing this ...

Someone who I would like to share my

feelings with is _____.

I will do this by talking to them / writing

them a note. (Circle one)

Dear _____,

Today I feel _____

because _____

_____

_____

_____

_____

_____

_____

_____

_____

_____

_____

_____

*The back of this page is left blank so that you can draw a picture of how you feel and tear this page out of your journal to give someone your message.

Date: _____

Today I feel _____.

This is a picture of how I'm feeling today ...

I feel this way because ...

_____

_____

_____

_____

_____

_____

_____

Something that might help me feel better is ...

_____

_____

_____

_____

_____

_____

Picture of me doing this ...

Someone who I would like to share my

feelings with is _____.

I will do this by talking to them / writing

them a note. (Circle one)

Dear _____,

Today I feel _____

because _____

_____

_____

_____

_____

_____

_____

_____

_____

_____

_____

_____

_____

*The back of this page is left blank so that you can draw a picture of how you feel and tear this page out of your journal to give someone your message.

Date: _____

Today I feel _____.

This is a picture of how I'm feeling today ...

I feel this way because ...

_____

_____

_____

_____

_____

_____

Something that might help me feel better is ...

_____

_____

_____

_____

_____

_____

Picture of me doing this ...

Someone who I would like to share my

feelings with is _____.

I will do this by talking to them / writing

them a note. (Circle one)

Dear _____,

Today I feel _____

because _____

_____

_____

_____

_____

_____

_____

_____

_____

_____

_____

_____

_____

The back of this page is left blank so that you can draw a picture of
ow you feel and tear this page out of your journal to give someone
our message.

Date: _____

Today I feel _____.

This is a picture of how I'm feeling today ...

I feel this way because ...

_____

_____

_____

_____

_____

_____

_____

_____

Something that might help me feel better is ...

_____

_____

_____

_____

_____

_____

Picture of me doing this ...

Someone who I would like to share my

feelings with is _____.

I will do this by talking to them / writing

them a note. (Circle one)

Dear _____,

Today I feel _____

because _____

_____

_____

_____

_____

_____

_____

_____

_____

_____

_____

_____

_____

The back of this page is left blank so that you can draw a picture of
how you feel and tear this page out of your journal to give someone
your message.

Date: _____

Today I feel _____.

This is a picture of how I'm feeling today ...

I feel this way because ...

_____

_____

_____

_____

_____

_____

_____

Something that might help me feel better is ...

_____

_____

_____

_____

_____

_____

Picture of me doing this ...

Someone who I would like to share my

feelings with is _____.

I will do this by talking to them / writing

them a note. (Circle one)

Dear _____,

Today I feel _____

because _____

_____

_____

_____

_____

_____

_____

_____

_____

_____

_____

_____

_____

*The back of this page is left blank so that you can draw a picture of
how you feel and tear this page out of your journal to give someone
your message.

Date: _____

Today I feel _____.

This is a picture of how I'm feeling today ...

I feel this way because ...

_____

_____

_____

_____

_____

_____

_____

Something that might help me feel better is ...

_____

_____

_____

_____

_____

_____

Picture of me doing this ...

Someone who I would like to share my

feelings with is _____.

I will do this by talking to them / writing

them a note. (Circle one)

Dear _____,

Today I feel _____

because _____

_____

_____

_____

_____

_____

_____

_____

_____

_____

_____

_____

_____

*The back of this page is left blank so that you can draw a picture of
how you feel and tear this page out of your journal to give someone
your message.

Made in the USA
Middletown, DE
28 July 2020